RUDY

AND THE

SECRET

SLEEPSKATER

This book is dedicated to Mia Mae & Bo Bo - P.W.

Dedicated to Zina, thanks for your support and enthusiasm! – G.E

OXFORD
UNIVERSITY PRESS

Great Clarendon Street, Oxford OX2 6DP
Oxford University Press is a department of the University of Oxford.
It furthers the University's objective of excellence in research, scholarship,
and education by publishing worldwide. Oxford is a registered trade mark
of Oxford University Press in the UK and in certain other countries

Text copyright © Paul Westmoreland 2023
Illustrations copyright © George Ermos 2023

The moral rights of the author have been asserted

Database right Oxford University Press (maker)

First published in 2023

British Library Cataloguing in Publication Data

Data available

ISBN: 978-0-19-278253-3

1 3 5 7 9 10 8 6 4 2

Printed in Great Britain by Bell and Bain Ltd, Glasgow

The manufacturing process conforms to the environmental
regulations of the country of origin.

MIX
Paper | Supporting
responsible forestry
FSC® C007785

RUDY AND THE

SECRET
SLEEPSKATER

WRITTEN BY
PAUL WESTMORELAND

PICTURES BY
GEORGE ERMOS

OXFORD
UNIVERSITY PRESS

RUDY
WEREWOLF

 Lives with:
Mum and Dad

 Likes: skateboarding,
pizza, adventure!

 Dislikes: baths

 Personality: brave,
impulsive, mischievous,
kind

 Best skateboard move:
The Daring Double!

FEMI MUMMY

- Lives with: Mum, Dad, Nan, and his three sisters—Raziya, Tabia, and Zahara
- Likes: skateboarding, biscuits, computer games
- Dislikes: pressure
- Personality: funny, loyal, slightly shy but the power of the pack brings out his confidence
- Best skateboard move: Riding the Vert Ramp!

EDIE GHOST

- Lives with: every member of her family tree and a whole host of others. The list is literally endless.
- Likes: BMXing, stating the obvious, spending time with her friends
- Dislikes: dishonesty
- Personality: confident, calm in a crisis, quick-witted
- Best BMX move: The Floating Flip!

CHAPTER
ONE

T he wind whipped Rudy's spiky hair as he sped down the vert ramp. It was the tallest ramp in the Skateway and got its name because it was vertical. Riding it was like skating down a cliff face!

If Rudy wasn't on his Pitbull-360, he'd be falling!

Down . . .

Down . . .

Down he hurtled in a speeding nose-dive, heading straight for the ground. Then the curve kicked in, his wheels glided in an arc, and he skidded to a stop.

'Whoo-ho!' Edie cheered from the top of the ramp, ringing the bell on her BMX:

TRING! TRING!

Wolfie let out a cub-sized howl and jumped up at Femi. He was up next. But as he eyed the sheer ramp, he became a bandaged bundle of jittery nerves.

'It's OK,' Edie reassured him. 'All you have to do is kick off and go for it—you'll be fine.'

'Oh, I don't know,' Femi said, recoiling.

'Hey, it's no big deal. You can do it!' Rudy said as he joined them. The adrenaline was still rushing through him. 'Just be confident.'

Femi gulped and started shaking.

'You'd better make up your mind,' Edie said, looking at her watch. 'It's nearly your dinner time.'

Femi looked like he'd been thrown a lifeline. 'Yeah, let's do this another day.'

'Really?' Rudy looked disappointed. 'We could ride it together?'

'That'd be great,' Femi said. 'But it's OK.'

'So long as you're sure.' Rudy shrugged.

Edie gave him a supportive smile. 'We'll all do it next time.'

The setting sun was turning a deep orange over Cobble Cross as they set off to go home.

'Are you both still coming to my sleepover tomorrow?' Femi asked.

'Yeah!' Rudy replied with eager excitement.

'Absolutely!' Edie said. 'Can't wait to see your house.'

'And your room,' Rudy added.

Femi looked relieved. 'Sorry you've had to wait so long. My parents like to plan these things.'

'That's OK.' Rudy smiled, and Edie nodded.

'It's gonna be great,' Femi continued. 'We can have a midnight feast with my mum's homemade biscuits. And I've got the new Rock Fortress game—it's amazing!'

'I am *soooo* looking forward to playing that!' Edie said.

'Yeah, it sounds awesome!' Rudy beamed as Wolfie pawed one of Femi's loose bandages.

'Ah!' Femi sighed as he remembered something. The bandages on his face couldn't hide his awkwardness. 'I'm really sorry, but Wolfie can't come.'

Rudy frowned. 'Why not? He's adorable!'

'It's not *him*,' Femi said, wringing his hands. 'It's my parents—they don't like pets.'

Rudy looked crestfallen. He hated the idea of Wolfie missing out on all the fun.

'Hey, it's their house,' Edie said with a shrug. 'They make the rules, Rudy.'

Rudy's parents hadn't liked the idea of having a pet wolf cub either, but he'd miss having Wolfie curled up on his bed at the sleepover. Rudy thought for a minute. 'Yeah, OK,' he agreed reluctantly.

By the time Rudy sat down to dinner, his disappointment was forgotten, and he was almost too excited about tomorrow night's sleepover to eat!

Femi was always fun to be around, so his house was bound to be awesome!

As exciting thoughts buzzed around Rudy's head, his mum and dad brought out dinner. It was a delicious roast chicken with piles of mashed potato—Rudy's favourite!

He dived straight in.

'Hey! Where are your manners, young man?' Dad scolded.

'Sorry,' Rudy replied and waited for his parents to sit down.

As soon as dinner was cleared away, Rudy checked the clock. He still had ages before bedtime.

'Mum, can I do some gaming?' he asked.

'Not after dinner. You know the rules,' came the reply he half-expected.

'Besides, you should get an early night,' Dad said. 'You don't want to be tired at your sleepover.'

Rudy sighed. Dad was probably right. He hugged his parents goodnight and went upstairs.

As Rudy climbed into his comfy bed, Wolfie looked subdued. 'You'll be OK. I'll only be gone one night,' he reassured the cub. 'And Femi's house isn't that far away. If you miss me, just send out a howl.'

Wolfie jumped up and rolled over, inviting Rudy to tickle his belly. Rudy immediately felt forgiven. They snuggled together while Rudy read until he was sleepy.

CHAPTER
TWO

Rudy spent the next day watching the clock until it was time to go to Femi's sleepover. When Dad's car pulled up outside, Rudy sprang out, bursting with excitement.

But Femi's house was not what he expected. Unlike Rudy's ramshackle home, it was a sweet little cottage. Instead of patches on the roof, they had skylights. The front lawn was mown in stripes you could measure with a ruler, and the flowerbeds were filled with pretty pink and yellow roses.

'Well, this looks lovely,' Dad said, impressed.

Rudy wondered, *Did his messy friend live here?* He double-checked the address, but this was the right place.

Dad handed Rudy his overnight bag. His bushy beard tickled as he kissed Rudy goodbye. 'Try not to have too much fun, OK!'

Rudy wanted to have fun, but he couldn't stop staring at Wolfie, wishing he didn't have to say goodbye.

'He'll be fine,' Dad said and ruffled Rudy's hair. 'C'mon son.'

Rudy stroked the cub. 'OK, see you tomorrow, Wolfie. Be good.'

Rudy waved as Dad drove away with Wolfie staring mournfully through the rear window. The sight made Rudy wonder, *How could he ever have agreed to leave him behind?*

But it was too late now. As the car turned off at the junction, two familiar voices called out, 'RUDY!'

He turned and saw Edie and Femi waving from the doorway.

Rudy pushed his doubts aside and hurried up the path. Femi greeted him with a hug on the doorstep.

'Welcome, Rudy!' Femi's dad said. He was tall and gangly. His neck bandage was knotted like a tie.

'Please come in,' Femi's mum said. Her kind smile shone through her bandages.

'Thanks!' Rudy smiled back.

Rudy squeezed into the narrow hallway and was met with more reminders that he was a long way from home.

Everything was as neat and tidy as the garden. The carpet was hoovered in stripes like the lawn, and every surface was home to delicate ornaments that looked like they would shatter if anyone sneezed.

The air was filled with smells that were unlike anything that had been up Rudy's nose before! As he breathed them in, his hackles rose and his nostrils went into overdrive trying to catch them all.

Rudy wanted to ask about the smells, but somewhere in the house, someone was shouting: '... *THEY'RE GUIDED BY WILD INSTINCTS!*'

'Dinner won't be long,' Femi's dad said over the loud voice.

'Why don't you say hello to Nan?' Femi's mum suggested.

Femi nodded. 'OK.'

Femi led his friends along the corridor.

As he opened the sitting room door, they were met with a ferocious

–RRAAARRRGGHHH!

The sound blew back Femi's bandages, and Edie's ghostly glow dimmed in fear. Rudy clamped his paws over his ears. It was so loud that he felt like his heightened hearing was being attacked by knitting needles.

Femi showed them in. Nan was sitting in an armchair with a blanket over her knees. She looked ancient and was watching TV with the volume turned up to the max.

'NAN!' Femi shouted. 'These are my friends, Rudy and Edie. They'd like to say hello.'

Nan's eyes stayed glued to the TV. 'Not now. This is important!' she barked.

'Typical!' Femi rolled his eyes and ushered his friends out of the room. 'We'd better leave her alone. Nan can be a bit funny when she's watching TV.'

'That's OK,' Edie said. 'I have a lot of *very* funny relatives.'

Rudy didn't have any funny relatives, but he wanted to make Femi feel better. 'Shall we play Rock Fortress?'

'Sorry,' Femi said, looking awkward. 'We need the TV and Nan's, well . . .'

'Oh, OK,' Rudy said, disappointed.

'I know!' Edie said. 'Let's help with dinner.'

'Yeah,' Rudy said, keen to have some fun.

As the kitchen door opened, clouds of smoky steam billowed out, and Rudy's sensitive nostrils took another hit. As his eyes watered, Rudy realized that the overpowering smells were coming from the dinner!

'We'd like to help,' Femi announced.

'Great,' replied Femi's dad. 'You can set the table.'

As they laid out the cutlery, Femi's three older sisters came in and sat down.

'This is Raziya, Tabia, and Zahara,' Femi's mum said.

They must've spent hours styling their bandages. Raziya's were in plaits. Tabia's were tied in a large bow on her head. And little Zahara's loose ends were sticking out like flower petals.

'Hello.' Rudy smiled.

'Ah! Perfect timing,' Femi's dad said as he brought out a platter of food. 'For starters, we have prawns glazed in sweet chilli sauce.'

Rudy couldn't believe his eyes as more dishes followed.

'This is a crab and clam salad dressed in cloves and cumin. These are Red Sea lobsters in a black pepper béarnaise sauce. And this is

my speciality, catfish katsu curry.'

The myriad of smells made Rudy wince, but they weren't done yet!

Femi's mum set down another dish. 'This is a rack of octopus tentacles fried with turmeric and tarragon.' Rudy couldn't believe it. The tentacles were even standing upright, curled like question marks!

'And in honour of our visitors . . .' Femi's dad announced.

Rudy was excited to see what he thought were . . . *'Scotch eggs?'*

'Not in this house!' remarked Raziya. 'We have proper food!'

'These are soft-boiled quails' eggs coated in a venison confit and French mustard,' Zahara explained as Rudy burnt with embarrassment.

'That's right. Nothing but the best for my prince and princesses.' Femi's dad smiled.

'Thank you, Pharaoh Daddy,' Tabia said.

'They're my favourite!' Femi beamed.

'And this is my favourite,' Femi's mum said. 'An ostrich-egg fondue. I've been boiling it for nearly an hour, and it's perfect. Help yourselves to breadsticks. They're blackened with squid ink!'

'This all looks amazing!' Edie said.

Rudy cast a nervous eye down the table and gulped. The fancy banquet wasn't exactly taking his fancy.

As everyone began taking dainty bites of the delicacies, Rudy recalled diving into his dinner last night and felt even worse!

'Aren't you hungry?' Femi's dad asked.

'I'm good, thanks.' Rudy smiled politely.

Thankfully, Edie wasn't eating either.

'Would you like some biscuits?' Femi's mum asked.

Rudy's eyes lit up. 'Yes please!'

She passed Rudy the tin, and he opened it. To his disappointment, the biscuits were stuffed with nutmeg and cinnamon and dusted with orange zest. The smell went straight up his nose and punched his brain!

'Ooh, they're fresh,' Femi said and winked.

Rudy winced.

Everyone was staring, so Rudy grabbed a handful. 'Thanks,' he said.

Femi's family stared, horrified as Rudy set the stack of biscuits on his plate.

'I'll err . . . save some for our midnight feast,' Rudy explained.

'How about you, Edie?' Femi's mum asked.

'I'm fine, thanks,' she replied. 'Dinner isn't really a thing in my house.'

'Of course.' Femi's mum nodded, remembering that ghosts don't eat.

'Do you know what's a thing in our house?' Raziya asked with a devilish grin.

Her sisters began to giggle, and the room filled with the sense that something was up!

There was a silent pause before Raziya answered her own question: *'Sleepwalking!'*

Rudy and Edie frowned.

Femi dropped his head in his hands to hide his embarrassment. But it was too late— his secret was out!

Tabia clapped her hands. 'Do you remember the night we thought we had burglars and caught Femi lapping water out of the fish tank?'

All the girls erupted with laughter, and Femi's embarrassment began to burn.

Rudy and Edie couldn't believe it.

They had no idea their friend was a secret sleepwalker!

'That wasn't as funny as the time we caught him serenading Nan's gnomes!' Raziya laughed, recalling the memory.

'That was shameful!' Tabia said.

Rudy had to admit it sounded pretty funny.

'Hey!' Zahara said. 'What about the time we found him on the lawn, skipping with his bandages?'

As everyone laughed, Femi tried to bury
himself under his bandages.

'I wish we had a photo of that!' giggled
Femi's dad.

'OK, that's enough,' Femi's mum said.
'Can't you see he's embarrassed?'

'We're only warning Femi's friends!'
Zahara sounded indignant.

'Yeah, if he sleepwalks tonight,' Tabia
said, 'just guide him back to bed.'

'And whatever happens,' Raziya was deadly serious, 'don't wake him up!'

Edie gasped.

Rudy's face froze. 'Why, what will happen?'

Femi didn't say anything.

'You don't want to know,' Zahara said.

'It doesn't bear thinking about,' Tabia added.

'OK,' Edie said. 'We'll take care of him.'

Rudy nodded. Although they both hoped they wouldn't have to!

CHAPTER
THREE

As everyone finished eating, Femi tilted his head towards the sitting room, and listened out. 'Hey, Nan's programme has finished. Shall we play Rock Fortress?'

'Yeah, I can't wait to see how you defeat the iron guards,' Edie said.

Rudy's excitement fired up. 'Can we really, please?'

'Sure, you still have half an hour before bedtime,' Femi's mum replied.

'Awesome! Thank you!' Rudy said.

Nan had already taken herself to bed. Her snoring was echoing along the corridor, so the sitting room was all theirs.

In no time, the game was loaded. Femi was Corell, a mercenary warrior, searching the catacombs beneath Rock Fortress for the lost relics that were needed to defeat the evil emperor Kardor Brazon and free Queen Mercia from the highest tower.

As Femi's fingers flew over the controls, Corell charged down the torchlit tunnels. Iron guards lunged out of the shadows. And with each flick of Femi's thumb, Corell's broadsword sliced across the screen

–SWISSSH-KLANG!

The guards disintegrated into rusty dust, and bags of gold leapt into Corell's backpack.

'That's easy,' Rudy said.

'Yeah, but you're missing the important stuff,' Edie said, pointing at the screen. 'Those scratches on the floor are from a secret door. Hit that brick.'

Femi did as Edie said and . . . 'Bingo!' he cried as it opened. 'That's Mantor's lost sword. Awesome!'

'Yeah. That's one of the five relics you need to defeat Kardor Brazon,' Edie explained.

'Cool!' Rudy said. 'Let's have a go?'

'Sure.' Femi paused the game and handed him the controls. 'You press this button to fight, this one to move forwards, this button to jump, and . . .'

'It's OK. I can do it,' Rudy said and set off through the tunnels.

But the moment he turned the first corner, the screen went black.

—CHA-CHING!

Two crossed swords appeared with the words 'GAME OVER'.

'Whoa! What happened there?' Rudy scowled.

'Ah, there's a poison pitfall around that corner,' Femi said.

'You need to turn and hit jump,' Edie said, pointing to the controls.

'Let me try it again,' Rudy said, and Femi reloaded the game.

This time, Rudy turned the corner and pressed jump. He caught a glimpse of a huge pile of treasure just before the screen went black.

—CHA-CHING!

—GAME OVER.

'Nooo!' Rudy exclaimed.

'It's OK. You'll do it,' Femi said.

Rudy tried again and again, but his claws kept slipping on the controls.

'This is impossible!' Rudy fumed.

'Why don't you let Femi show you what to do?' Edie said.

'OK,' Rudy sighed.

In a couple of swift taps, Femi had

leapt over the poison pitfall and bagged the treasure. 'See, it's no big deal. You can do it,' Femi said.

Rudy was about to have another go when Femi's mum popped in and said, 'OK, bedtime. You'd better get some sleep before your midnight feast.'

Rudy had expected the sleepover to be awesome, but so far it had been one disappointment after another. And he was so annoyed, he didn't brush his teeth—he scrubbed them!

—SUSSH-SUSSH-SUSSH!

Not being allowed to bring Wolfie was bad enough. Then Femi's nan scared him. The house had so many smells Rudy was worried his nose might never recover. And they ate like royalty, which made Rudy feel

like an animal!

Even playing Rock Fortress was impossible. The fact it was awesome only added to his frustrations.

He was about to throw down his toothbrush when his hackles shot up. The feeling took him by surprise. It usually meant . . .

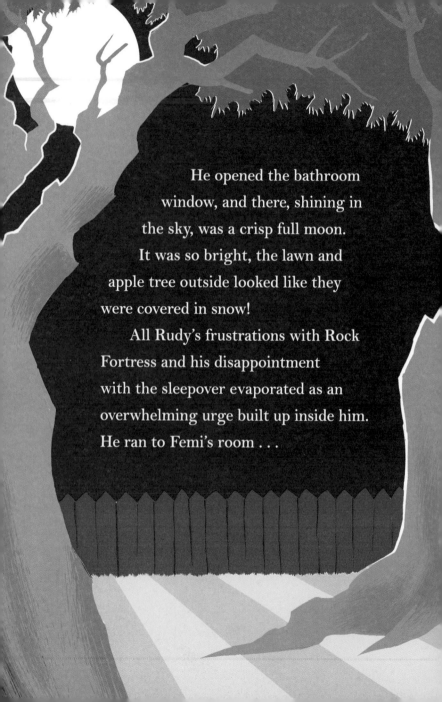

He opened the bathroom
window, and there, shining in
the sky, was a crisp full moon.
It was so bright, the lawn and
apple tree outside looked like they
were covered in snow!

All Rudy's frustrations with Rock
Fortress and his disappointment
with the sleepover evaporated as an
overwhelming urge built up inside him.
He ran to Femi's room . . .

'Hey, guys! It's a full moon! Let's go out and howl at it,' he said.

'Really?' Edie asked, sitting up from her sleeping bag on the floor.

'Are you sure?' Femi asked. He looked comfy in his bed as he set the alarm on his watch for their midnight feast.

'Yeah, we always do it at my house,' Rudy said.

'Oh,' Femi's voice wobbled. He didn't want to disappoint Rudy, but . . . 'My parents don't really like me going out late,' he said.

'We'll only go onto the roof,' Rudy promised, pointing at the skylight.

Femi still wasn't sure. 'But howling might wake up Nan. She can get really upset if she's disturbed.'

'Oh, OK.' Rudy sighed, giving in to yet another disappointment.

Rudy climbed into his sleeping bag and yanked the zip shut. Even the midnight feast didn't appeal now!

'Night,' Femi said with a yawn and flicked off the light. Inky darkness filled the room.

Rudy tried to settle down, but the floor was as hard as a gravestone. He missed his comfy bed and having Wolfie curled up by his feet. He was beginning to wish he'd stayed at home!

Rudy sighed and rolled over. To his surprise, there was Edie. 'BOO!' she said.

'*WAH!*' Rudy nearly jumped out of his sleeping bag.

'What was that?' Femi sat bolt upright.

'Sorry, couldn't resist it,' Edie giggled. 'I'm not sleepy yet.'

'Me neither,' Rudy said.

'I'm wide awake now, too!' Femi said.

'Would you like to hear a ghost story?' Edie asked.

Rudy nodded. Despite all the disappointments, he couldn't turn down the chance to hear a real ghost tell a ghost story!

As the boys got comfy, Edie began.

'Long ago, there were two ghosts who, in their own special ways, loved to make mischief.

'Kyle would hide inside the tiniest nook and wait for hours, days even, to jump out and terrify anyone he caught unawares.

'Vermour liked to set traps and laughed hysterically when someone tripped and fell on their face.

'Their love of mischief made them the best of friends.

'One day, a greedy old developer bought the house Kyle haunted with a plan to demolish it and build some flats.

'Kyle was livid. So he invited Vermour to move in so that together they could make enough mischief to scare away the developer.

'Vermour happily agreed, and while he set his traps, Kyle looked for somewhere to hide. He looked under the stairs, in the fridge, and even down the toilet. Finally, Kyle hid in a teapot so he could jump out and scare the developer when he put the kettle on.

'And so they waited . . .

'Eventually, the developer arrived. The moment he stepped inside, an old floorboard nail stuck in his foot.

'*"OWWWW!"* he cried.

'He started hobbling upstairs to the bathroom where there was a medical cabinet. But Vermour had loosened the stair carpet too. Halfway up, the developer tripped and started falling down the stairs.

'K-DUNK!

'K-THWACK!

'K-THUNK!

'But that wasn't all. Vermour had also
tied a loose thread from the carpet to an old
moose's head that was hanging on the wall.

'As the developer tumbled down the
stairs, the thread pulled the moose's head off
the wall and bounced it after him.

'BOOMP!

'BROINK!

'DONK!

'When the developer landed in a heap, the moose's head fell on top of him, and its antler stuck in his bum!

'"*ARRGH!*"

'Vermour couldn't contain himself.

'"*HA! HA! HA! HAAAAA!*"

'As his laughter echoed through the house, the terrified developer jumped up and ran out, clutching his bum, never to be seen again.

'Vermour laughed so hard, Kyle came to see what was going on.

"*HA-HAA!* I tricked you too," Vermour laughed.

'Kyle was bitterly disappointed. He hated missing out as much as Vermour liked playing tricks. And this was supposed to be fun!

'As he listened to Vermour's laughter, Kyle realized something—they were too

different to be friends after all. So he vowed
to scare Vermour out of the house!

'And to this day, those two ghosts are
still locked in an eternal battle, scaring and
tricking each other for mischievous revenge!

'So be warned, sometimes living
with your best friend can turn out to be a
nightmare!'

CHAPTER
FOUR

By the time Edie had finished her story, the only sounds left in the house were Nan's reverberating snores.

Femi was fast asleep too, the bandages over his nose flapping slightly with each breath.

'Goodnight, Rudy,' Edie said and settled into her sleeping bag.

'Night,' Rudy whispered. He tried to settle down too, but something was refusing to let him sleep.

From the moment he arrived, something hadn't felt right. With each disappointment,

Rudy's unease had grown, and now awkwardness was crawling all over him like ants.

As Rudy lay there in the darkness, he began to wonder if he and Femi were like the two ghosts in Edie's story.

Femi had always been fun to hang out with, but the sleepover had been so disappointing that Rudy was beginning to wonder, *Are Femi and me too different to be friends, after all?*

As this train of thought ran away, it left Rudy feeling even worse.

He rolled over and let out a sigh. A glimmer of moonlight was shining through a gap in the blinds drawn over the skylight. It seemed to whisper to Rudy, calling him with the strength of a piercing howl.

But he wasn't allowed out!

Rudy buried his head under his pillow.

But he could still hear Nan's snoring, and every fibre of his body wanted to go out there—out onto the roof—and send his biggest howl all the way to the moon, just like he would if he were at home.

He imagined Wolfie with his mum and dad, howling on their patched-up old roof without him.

Howling at the moon always felt great, and it was a lot more fun than lying on a hard floor listening to an ancient mummy snoring!

Rudy threw back his pillow. The moonlight was still calling to his instincts.

Would a few howls really hurt anyone?

Besides, everyone was asleep now, so they wouldn't miss him. And if they could sleep through Nan's snoring, his howling wouldn't wake them up!

Rudy got up, climbed on a chair, and carefully opened the skylight.

Moonlight shone down on Rudy like a spotlight, encouraging him to perform.

In a few seconds, he was on the roof. The night air was cool and fresh. He tipped his head back, took a deep breath, and let out an enormous:

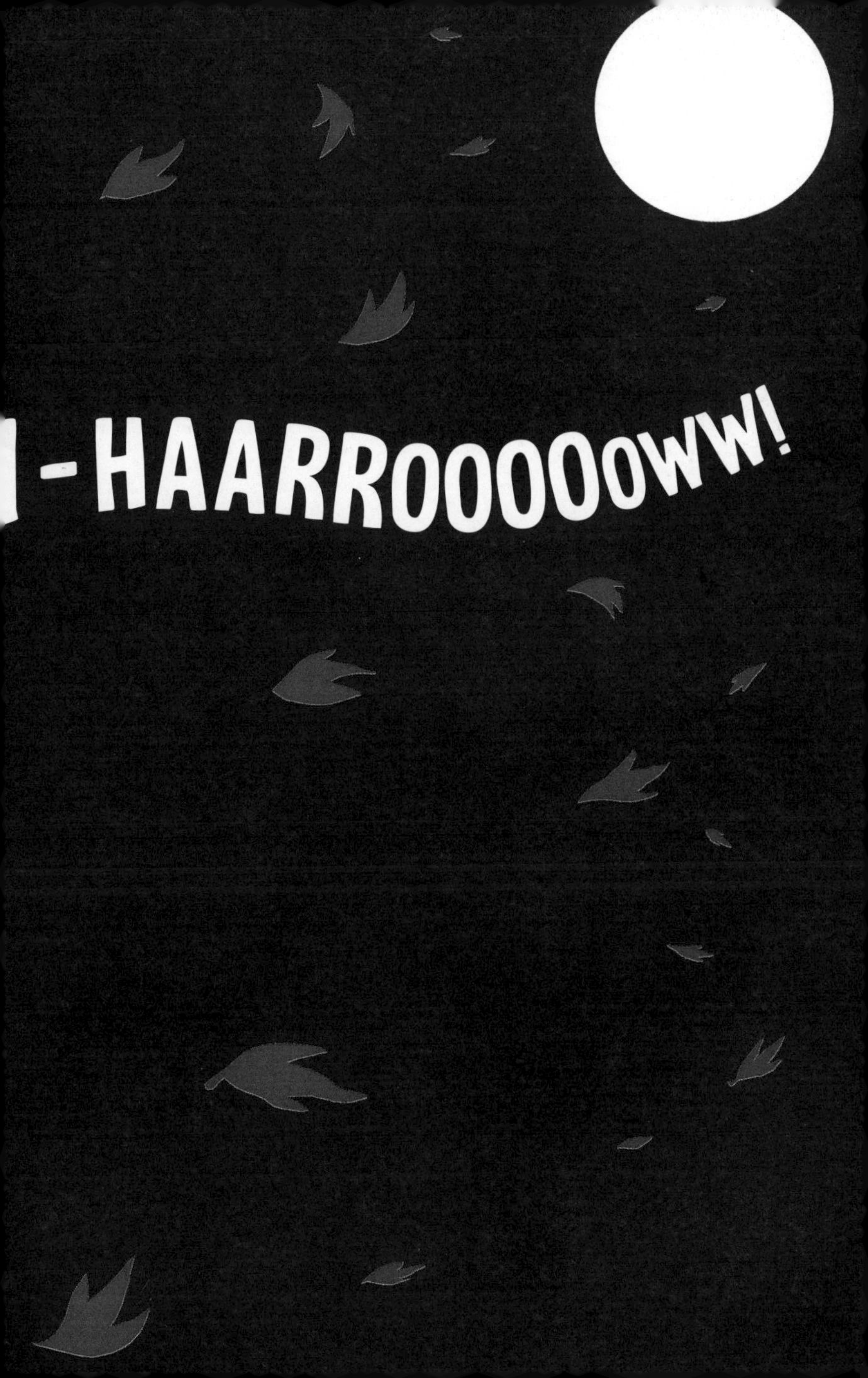
-HAARROOOOOOWW!

Rudy's howl sailed up, up towards the moon. He let out a sigh of relief, and a gentle calm feeling covered him like the moonlight.

As the night breeze gently rustled the leaves of the nearby apple tree, something in the distance made Rudy's ears prick up.

It was a howl!

One that Rudy knew very well.

He didn't need to hear it twice to know it was Wolfie!

Rudy tipped back his head . . .

He was about to unleash another howl when Edie floated up through the roof tiles.

'WAAH!'

The sudden sight of her made Rudy nearly fall off the roof!

'What are you doing?' she asked.

'I was just howling to Wolfie,' Rudy replied, trying to sound innocent.

'Seriously?' Edie frowned. 'You know Femi's parents wouldn't like you coming out here!'

'Yeah, but they won't know,' Rudy said, unable to hold her stare.

'You still shouldn't do it!' Edie said.

'I know.' Rudy sighed. 'But this place, it just doesn't feel . . .' his words trailed off.

'Like *home?*' Edie asked, raising an eyebrow.

'Yeah!' Rudy said. 'See, you get it!'

'Sure.' Edie shrugged. 'This isn't like my home either. All our homes are different.'

'True, but I thought this would at least be fun.' Rudy gazed down at the gritty roof tiles. 'I've been wondering . . . I know we both love skateboarding, but maybe Femi and I aren't really meant to be friends?'

Edie stared at Rudy in disbelief. 'Wow! I thought you'd just snuck out. I wasn't expecting *that!*'

'Neither was I.' Rudy nodded. 'I thought this sleepover would be awesome, but I can't sleep on his floor, eat his dinner or play his games! I just want to go home.'

'Hey, sleep on it. You might feel differently in the morning.' Edie grinned as an idea struck her. 'I know! Let's have a game of hide-and-seek. That'll tire you out.'

To cheer up her friend, Edie offered to count first, and Rudy climbed off the roof to find somewhere to hide.

Femi's garden was lined with shrubs, but none of them were big enough for Rudy to hide behind.

As he looked around, Edie counted, 'Five . . . Six . . . Seven . . .'

The apple tree!

It was perfect. The branches were

low and covered in leaves that wouldn't just hide Rudy, they'd camouflage him!

Rudy shimmied up, found a branch that could take his weight, and settled down.

It didn't take Edie long to search the shrubs.

'Found you!' she cried as she floated up into the apple tree.

'OK! I'll count now!' Rudy said.

As Rudy covered his eyes, Edie drifted away.

'. . . Nine . . . Ten!'

When Rudy jumped out of the tree, Edie was nowhere to be seen.

The moonlight gave Rudy a long, deep shadow as he crept across the lawn. He snuck up on the shrubs and pulled them apart. But Edie wasn't there.

He decided to try the front yard. As he tiptoed past Nan's window, her snores rattled the pane.

Rudy scoured the flowerbeds and looked up and down the street. There wasn't so much as a piece of litter. He even checked the dustbins. But Edie had vanished.

He was about to give up when he heard someone giggle.

Rudy looked around, half-expecting to catch Edie sneaking up on him.

But all he saw was the solid wall of the house.

As Rudy frowned, Edie leant out of the brickwork. 'Give up?' She smirked.

'Aw, you can't hide *inside* a wall!' Rudy said. 'That's not fair!'

'Yes, it is!' Edie replied. 'It's not my fault I'm a champion hide-and-seeker!'

Rudy laughed. There were many downsides to being a ghost, so he couldn't begrudge her one benefit.

'Are you sleepy yet?' Edie yawned.

Rudy was about to reply when something landed above them with a heavy:

—TH-UNNK!

They looked up and, to their horror, saw Femi was striding across the roof.

'Did we wake him?' Edie asked. 'Or is it time for our midnight feast?'

'Neither.' Rudy swallowed nervously as Femi took a step towards the guttering on the edge of the roof. 'He's sleepwalking!'

CHAPTER
FIVE

The joists let out a creaky whine as Femi's foot rose off the edge of the roof.

Rudy and Edie stared aghast. Their jaws dropped as Femi's bandaged foot wavered in mid-air.

Femi's sisters had been very clear: '*Just guide him back to bed.*' . . . '*And whatever happens, don't wake him up.*'

And now, thanks to Rudy's desire to howl at the moon, Femi was about to crash-dive into the lawn!

As Femi's foot came down, Rudy rushed forward, desperate to save him.

But it was too late.

Femi fell forward and tumbled into the air. As he closed in on the dewy grass, one of his bandages caught on a branch of the apple tree and yanked him back up into the air.

A wave of relief hit Rudy—he had another chance to avert disaster!

But instead of delivering the slumbering mummy safely into Rudy's waiting arms, the branch pinged back, swinging Femi like a ragdoll, and catapulted him over the house!

Rudy and Edie gawped in dismay as their friend flew across the sky, travelling even further and faster than Rudy's howl!

They ran to the front of the house in such a fearful panic, Rudy didn't worry about waking Nan!

They expected to find Femi lying in a heap of his bandages. Instead, he'd landed on his skateboard and was rolling away down the garden path!

'He's still sleepwalking!' Edie exclaimed.

'No,' Rudy said, 'he's sleep*skating!*'

And sure enough, he was!

Each time Femi took a step, he pushed off the ground and picked up speed . . .

In two steps, Femi burst through the garden gate and into the road.

'Come on!' Rudy shouted, wishing he hadn't left his Pitbull-360 at home! 'We have to guide him back to bed. It doesn't bear thinking about what'll happen if he wakes up .'

The pair of them gave chase as Femi raced off down the street.

Femi passed the neighbour's cat sitting on a wall. But it just watched him go by, totally unmoved, as though a sleepwalking mummy riding a skateboard was the sort of thing that happened every night!

As Femi approached the junction, Rudy's hackles rose, focussing his mind. He stopped running and tipped his head back.

He was about to howl when Edie hissed. 'Stop! You'll wake him!'

'We can't catch him,' Rudy replied. 'But Wolfie might!'

Edie's face crumpled with worry as Femi wheeled across the junction and headed off towards Maplestone Park. 'OK,' she nodded. 'Be quick.'

Rudy let out a loud,

A moment later, Wolfie hared out of the bushes, and the three of them continued their chase.

When they reached Maplestone Park, Femi was heading for the duckpond.

Rudy braced himself to watch his

friend make a splash-landing. But as Femi took another sleepy step, he kicked off a paving stone and began skipping over the ornamental stepping stones, like a pebble skimming a lake.

He made it to the far side with a skidding scrape of his wheels and skated away through the park.

'Quick!' Edie said, and they hurried after him. 'He's going to wreck the crazy-golf course!'

'Well, if he crashes into something, at least he's already bandaged up!'

'That is *NOT* helpful, Rudy!' Edie snapped.

As Femi tore across the course, Wolfie caught up with him and took a swipe at his flapping bandages. But it was no use, Femi was just too fast for him.

He skipped the first five holes and careered up the humpback bridge. At the top, his board took flight, and he fired into the air.

Edie gasped as Femi sailed over the windmill, and Rudy shouted, 'FOUR!'

Femi landed and made a beeline for the bushes.

Rudy felt sure the brambles would catch him and they'd spend the rest of the night untangling Femi's bandages from the thorns.

But Femi was going so fast that he barged through the bushes like a raging rhino!

'Oh no!' Edie called out. 'That way leads to the railway line!'

'Yeah!' Rudy gasped.

He frantically crawled under the bushes as Edie floated through them. They found Femi, clattering down the siding steps:

—DUG-GA!

—DUG-GA!

—DUG-GA!

Rudy listened carefully. Luckily, there was no sound of any distant trains. But that didn't mean there wouldn't be any soon!

Femi shot off the steps. Edie winced as he hit the tracks. But Femi took it in his sleepy stride and made a perfect rail slide along the track!

Rudy would've been impressed, but as Femi reached the level crossing, a horn blared out of nowhere:

–HURR-*URRRGH!*

Rudy's heart froze with fear.

As Femi's wheels hit the tarmac, a speeding taxi thundered through the crossing. Femi twisted, swerving and just missing the taxi, then spun away down the road.

Rudy realized he had been holding his breath and exhaled with relief. He and Wolfie were getting tired now, but Edie wouldn't let them rest. 'Come on, we can't give up!' she said, waving her arms encouragingly.

'We're coming,' Rudy replied as they sprinted across the level crossing.

A short distance away, they found Femi circling the roundabout.

'Oh, thank goodness,' Rudy said, catching his breath. He positioned himself on the road, ready to grab Femi by the bandages.

But as Femi approached, he kicked off the road and his board turned . . .

Edie gulped.

Wolfie yapped.

Rudy couldn't believe it! 'That's Downsway Hill!' he cried as Femi sped away, and all three of them started sprinting after him.

Downsway Hill wasn't just the steepest in Cobble Cross, it was notorious. The only thing steeper was the vert ramp. And now Femi was about to sleepskate down it!

Edie and Rudy could only watch in horror as Femi rattled over the ridge and plummeted away into the darkness.

Rudy felt awful. *Could this be the last they saw of Femi?*

He couldn't bear that thought. And it was all his fault for leaving the skylight open!

When they reached the bottom of the hill, there was no sign of Femi.

Rudy listened out . . . Nothing . . . Not a whisper. So he and Wolfie started sniffing out Femi's scent.

His trail wasn't hard to find, and it led them around the corner to the Skateway. As a nearby church struck midnight, an alarm rang out through the night:

—BEEP! BEEP! BEEP!

The sound hurt Rudy's ears, and a chilling shock swept over them as they looked up to see Femi teetering at the top of the vert ramp!

'FEMI!' Rudy cried out. He knew he shouldn't wake him, but anything was better than letting his friend fall to his death! And Femi's watch alarm was useless.

Femi's board wavered as his bandaged foot rose to take another step.

As Rudy ran to the top of the ramp, Wolfie bounded past him. The little cub took another swipe at Femi's bandages and hooked them with his claws.

'STOP!' Edie yelled as she floated in front of Femi.

But all he did was put his foot down and push off from the ramp!

'For the power of the pack!' Rudy cried and dived after his friend.

Edie dived after him too.

Air rushed around Rudy as Femi set off down the ramp.

And, with a yank of his bandages, Wolfie was pulled along too!

Rudy's eyes opened wide with terror as he started falling.

The only sound was Femi's spinning wheels scraping against the concrete.

Rudy reached out. He felt the fabric of Femi's bandages. He grabbed his friend's shoulders and pulled him close. And together they all skated down the ramp.

-VVEERRROOOOSSH!

It was a rushing, whizz of adrenaline-fuelled excitement. The kind that usually made Rudy want to do this all over again. But as the board followed an arc around and came to a stop, all Rudy could think about was getting Femi back home.

'Well done!' Edie said, beaming.

'Yeah, we did good.' Rudy grinned as Femi's head rested on Rudy's shoulder and he started snoring.

As they began pushing their sleepy friend home, Rudy's tummy couldn't help rumbling.

'Sounds like you need a midnight feast,' Edie said.

Rudy's face lit up as he remembered the biscuits he took at dinner. He'd put them in his pyjama pocket. He hadn't fancied them then, but after all that running he could eat anything!

To Rudy's surprise, they were amazing. Wolfie loved them too. Before long, they were all gone, and the friends were back at the junction on Femi's road.

Rudy ruffled Wolfie's ears. 'I'm sorry, mate. You have to go home now. Femi's parents have rules, you know.' He shrugged.

Wolfie licked the biscuit crumbs off Rudy's fingers.

'Tell you what, I'll bring you some more

of those bad boys,' Rudy said, winking.

Wolfie seemed to understand and scampered off home.

'Come on.' Edie yawned as Rudy watched Wolfie go. 'We should all get to bed.'

CHAPTER SIX

When Rudy awoke, his sleeping bag felt warm and cosy. As he rolled over and saw the sunlight pouring through the skylight, the events of last night rushed back to him.

Rudy sat up in shock!

Thankfully, Femi was sleeping safely in his bed. But there was no escaping the fact that he'd broken Femi's parents' rules, and his friend had been in real danger, sleepskating around town.

A torrent of guilt hit Rudy so hard that he felt sick!

Femi sat up. His bones clicked as he

stretched and let out an exhausted yawn.

Rudy cringed, and Edie gave him a knowing look.

'I'm starving,' Femi said. 'Who's for breakfast?'

Femi's sisters were already in the kitchen when Rudy, Femi, and Edie arrived.

'Morning,' Femi's mum said, smiling.

'Did you sleep well?' Femi's dad asked.

'I'm more tired than when I went to bed,'
Femi said, letting out another big yawn.

'Been sleepwalking again?' Raziya
giggled, and the others laughed.

'Who knows?' Femi shrugged.

Rudy's guilt opened up like a whirlpool
in his stomach. It was too much.

'No, he hasn't,' Rudy blurted. 'He was
sleep*skating.*'

Everyone stared at him.

'It was all my fault,' Rudy continued. 'There was a full moon last night, so I sneaked out to howl at it. I know it was against your rules—I just needed to. Then I left the skylight open and Femi got out.'

'He sleepwalked on the roof?' Tabia asked, and Zahara gasped.

'Yeah,' Edie nodded. 'But he didn't fall . . . the apple tree threw him over the house onto his skateboard.'

'Wow! Where did he go?' Raziya asked.

'To err . . . the Skateway,' Rudy said, shame-faced.

Everyone gasped.

'Via the duckpond, the crazy-golf course, and the railway line,' Edie added.

Femi gulped.

His parents were horrified.

'But we brought him home safely,' Edie added.

'Yeah,' Rudy said. 'I was so scared we wouldn't see you again—the whole thing made me realize how much our friendship means to me.'

Femi looked slightly puzzled.

'I'm sorry,' Rudy continued. 'It's just, last night everything here felt really awkward. I thought your house would be like mine, but it isn't. Dinner was, well, different to what I'm used to. And I was so disappointed that I couldn't bring Wolfie, be any good at Rock Fortress, or go out and howl . . .

'Then Edie's ghost story made me wonder if we were even meant to be friends. But last night proved more than anything that we are. And while the things we have in common—like skating—bring us together, understanding our differences is what makes us real friends. And that's what we are. *Real friends.*'

Femi beamed. 'Yes, of course, we are!'

'For the power of the pack!' Rudy, Femi, and Edie said together and made a fist bump.

Rudy felt a huge sense of relief wash over him.

Edie said, 'Are you going to tell him about the vert ramp?'

Femi looked up.

'Oh yeah,' Rudy said. 'We rode it, together. With a little help from Wolfie.'

'*Really?!*' Femi was ecstatic.

'Yeah! I knew you could do it!' Rudy smiled.

'Well, I can't wait to do it again—with my eyes open!' Femi grinned.

'I wish we'd seen that!' Zahara said.

'Yeah, wake us up next time!' Raziya added.

'I'm amazed you didn't wake him,' Tabia said.

'Yeah,' Edie replied, nodding.

'What would've happened if we had woken him up?' Rudy asked, feeling slightly nervous.

'Oh, it's awful,' said Zahara, cringing.

'Yeah, he gets in a right mood!' said Raziya.

'Oh, is that all?' Edie said.

'Yeah, you really had us worried,' Rudy added, slightly embarrassed.

'Well, thank goodness everything turned out OK,' Femi's mum said.

As relieved as Rudy was, he still had one more thing to say. 'I'm really sorry I snuck out to howl at the moon.'

Femi's dad took a deep breath, and a stern frown covered his face.

Rudy thought he was for it now.

'You can't tell him off for *howling!*' bellowed a voice from the doorway.

Everyone turned to see Nan. She pointed at Rudy. 'He's a wolf boy—howling's natural to him. They don't call it a *wolf moon* for nothing.'

Femi's dad looked like he was being told off. 'How do you know that?'

'It was in my nature documentary. I told you it was important. You're never too old

to learn about other folk,' Nan said and sat down.

'OK.' Femi's dad smiled at Rudy. 'What would you like for breakfast?'

'Could I have some more of your biscuits, please? They were delicious. Wolfie loved them too.'

Femi's mum was pleased and passed him the tin. 'I'll give you the recipe if you like?'

'Yes, please!' Rudy nodded.

After several levels of Rock Fortress, Rudy got the hang of it. Then his dad arrived to pick him up. The moment the front door opened, Wolfie jumped up, excited to see Rudy.

As pleased as Rudy was to see the little cub, he also felt sad that his visit to Femi's house was over. Despite the disappointing start, it had turned out to be a lot of fun.

He gave his friend a warm hug as everyone crowded into the narrow corridor to wave him off. Even Nan was there. Wolfie playfully ran around everyone's ankles. He didn't know whose bandages to chase first!

'Thanks for the sleepover,' Rudy said.

'You're welcome, anytime,' Femi's mum replied, and a happy smile spread across Rudy's face. Femi's family were kind and truly special, and even though they did things differently, Rudy now knew that underneath their bandages, they all had the same power of the pack.

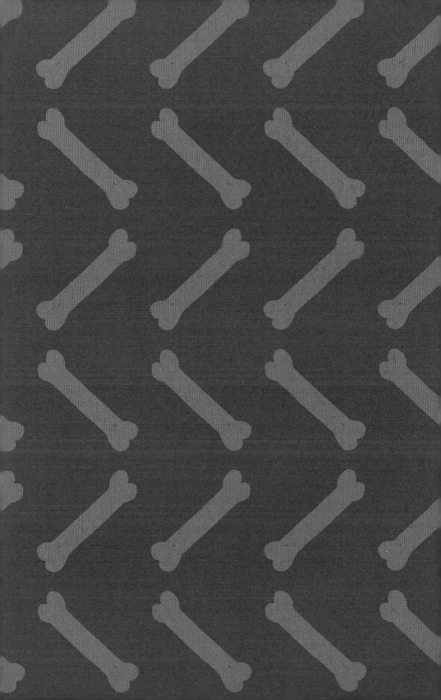

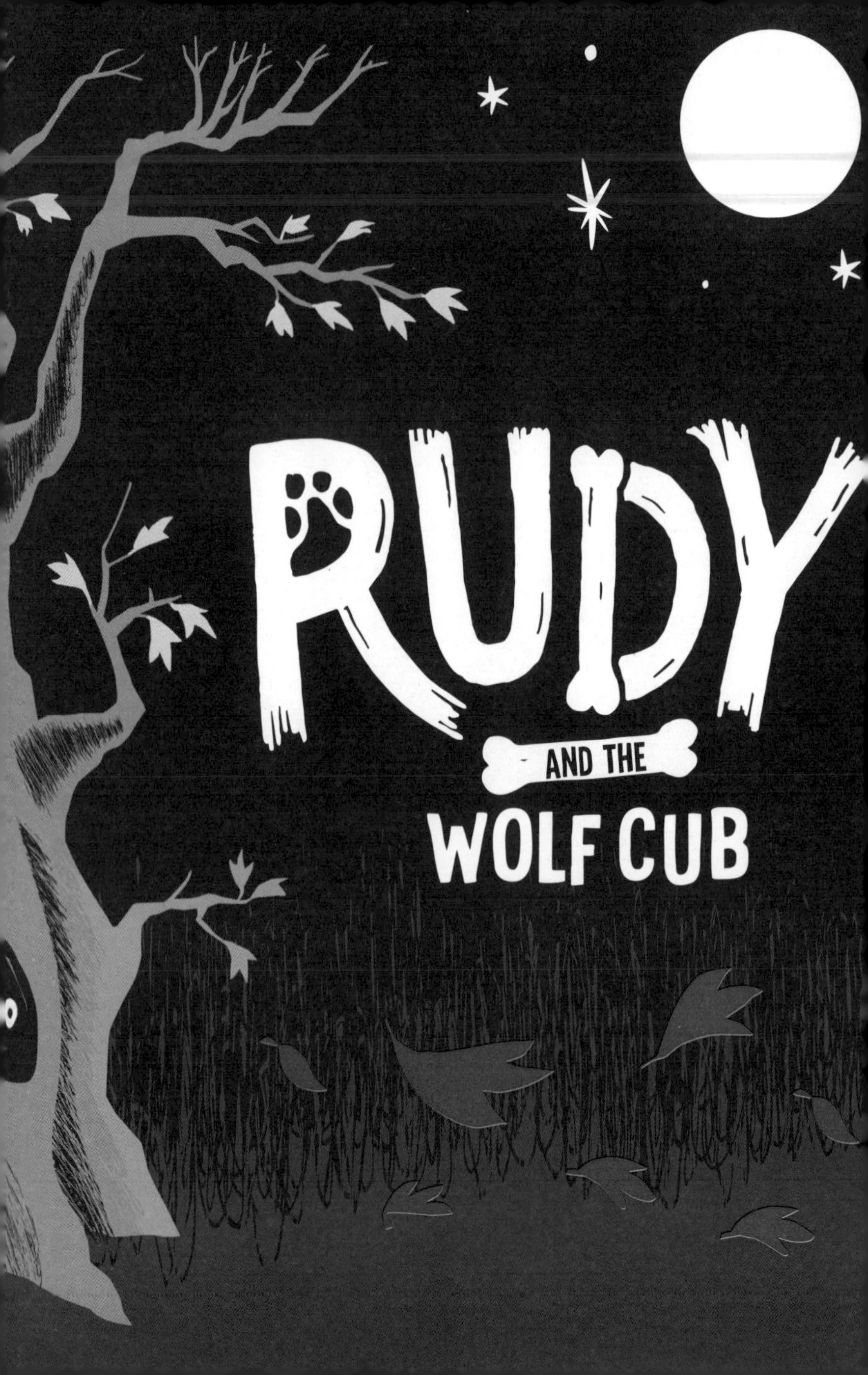
RUDY
AND THE
WOLF CUB

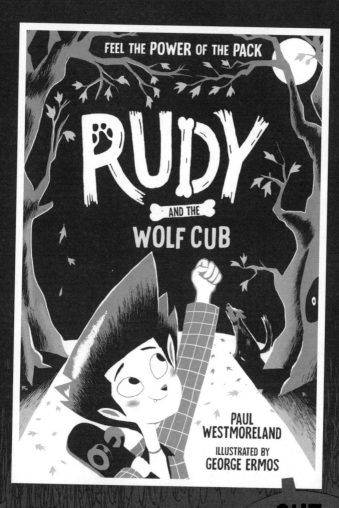

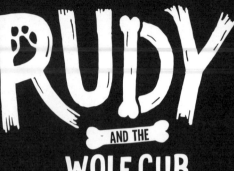

RUDY
AND THE
WOLF CUB

When Rudy finds a lost wolf cub at the
skatepark, he knows he has to help him.
Rudy tries everything he can think of to
find the cub's pack, but they're nowhere to
be seen, or smelled, and time is running out.
Can a howl in the night change the fate of
the little cub?

HOW-HOW-HAARROOOOWW!

A shiver scurried up Rudy's neck and Wolfie stopped in his tracks. 'Hey, it's all right,' Rudy reassured the cub, though it was mainly for his own benefit. 'If your pack are going to be anywhere, they'll be here. We just have to keep looking.'

Rudy tipped his head to one side and listened. All he could hear was the wind brushing the dry leaves.

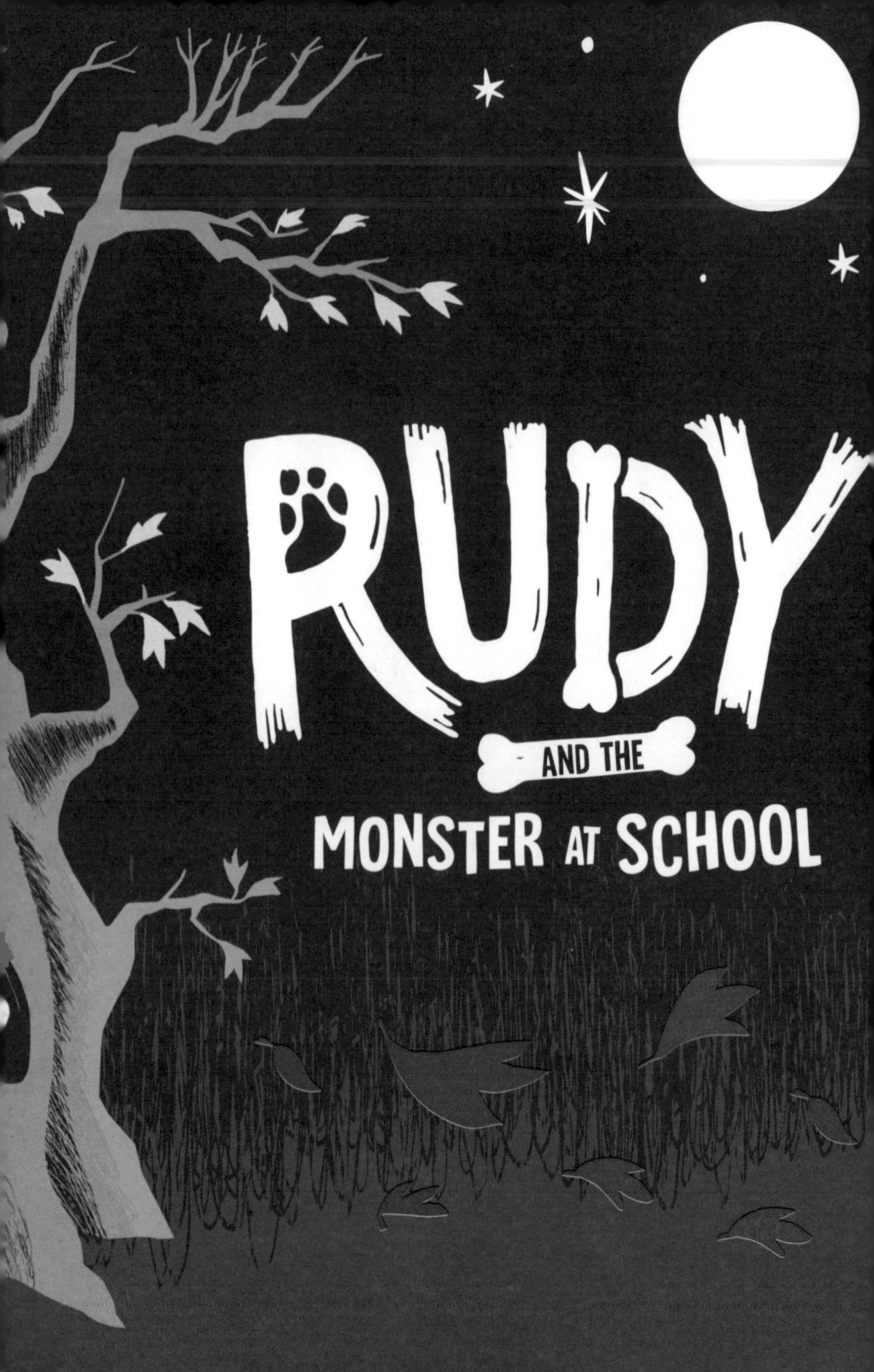
RUDY
AND THE
MONSTER AT SCHOOL

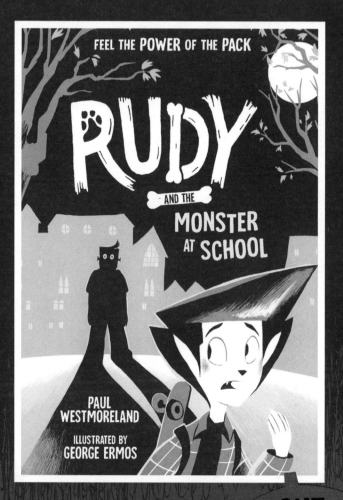

FEEL THE **POWER** OF THE PACK

RUDY

AND THE

MONSTER
AT SCHOOL

**PAUL
WESTMORELAND**

ILLUSTRATED BY
GEORGE ERMOS

**OUT
NOW**

RUDY

AND THE

MONSTER AT SCHOOL

There's a new boy in Rudy's school called
Frankie, and everyone says he is SCARY.
Which is really saying something, as Rudy's
class is full of ghosts and ghouls, and his
teacher is a vampire. But when Frankie gets
upset and runs away, Rudy knows he has to
help him. The trouble is, Rudy's wolf senses
lead him towards the really spooky castle
on the hill. Is Rudy brave enough to follow
his nose and find out the truth behind the
monster at school?

revealing an old abandoned castle, high up on the summit of the craggy rock.

Femi almost jumped out of his bandages. Wolfie let out a whimper. And Edie's ghostly aura dwindled like she was trying to disappear.

'That's High Crag Castle!' Femi wailed. 'We should turn back.'

They'd come a long way, but as Rudy faced up to the dangerous walk that lay ahead, he felt inclined to agree with his friend.

His feet turned, grinding on the gritty path.

'Hey!' Edie said, drifting in front of him. 'You said you wanted to apologize to Frankie. Have you changed your mind?'

'No,' Rudy replied, a little wounded.

'And Frankie's up there?' Edie asked.

Rudy nodded. 'That's where he lives!'

ABOUT THE
AUTHOR

I write about Rudy and his friends from a quiet room in my home, tucked away in South London. To say I love it is an understatement. It's almost as much fun as actually going on the adventures with Rudy, or hanging out with his friends at the Skateway. Although Rudy is a much better skateboarder than I am! If you love his stories, give me a

HOW-HOW-HAARROOOOWW!

ABOUT THE
ILLUSTRATOR

George is an illustrator, maker, and
avid reader from Derbyshire. He works
digitally and loves illustrating all things
curious and mysterious.

LOVE RUDY?
WHY NOT TRY THESE TOO . . .